Ashley Wolff

Only the Cat Saw

Dodd, Mead & Company
New York

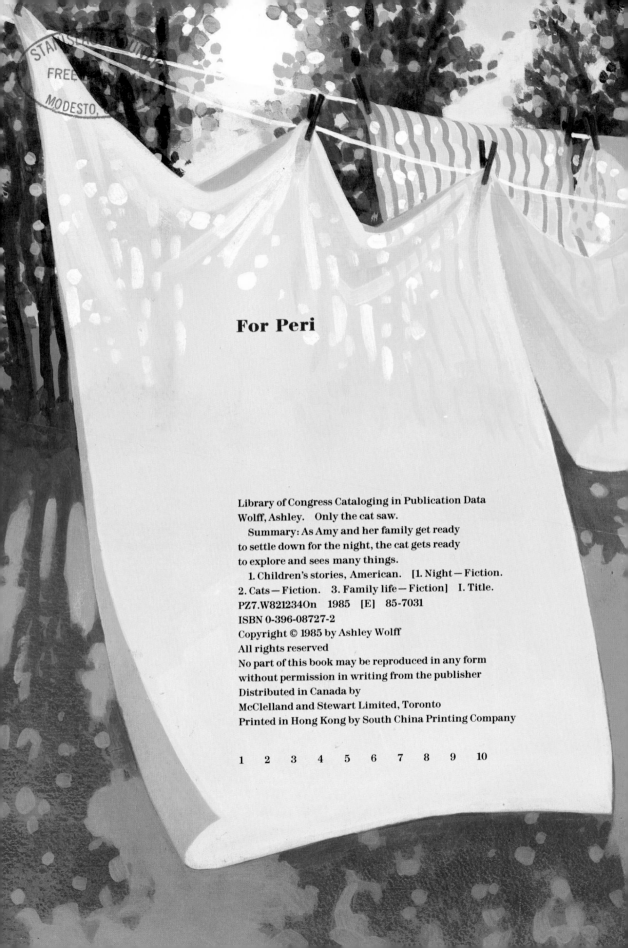

For Peri

Library of Congress Cataloging in Publication Data
Wolff, Ashley.   Only the cat saw.
   Summary: As Amy and her family get ready
to settle down for the night, the cat gets ready
to explore and sees many things.
   1. Children's stories, American.   [1. Night — Fiction.
2. Cats — Fiction.   3. Family life — Fiction]   I. Title.
PZ7.W821234On   1985   [E]   85-7031
ISBN 0-396-08727-2
Copyright © 1985 by Ashley Wolff

Distributed in Canada by
McClelland and Stewart Limited, Toronto
Printed in Hong Kong by South China Printing Company

1   2   3   4   5   6   7   8   9   10

It was suppertime
and night was coming soon.
Mother was busy with Sam.
Amy was helping Father.
So only the cat saw...

At bath time

Father was singing to Sam.

Mother was tickling Amy.

So only the cat saw...

At bedtime

Mother and Father were reading.

Sam was finally asleep, and

Amy was supposed to be.

So only the cat saw...

At midnight
Amy was dreaming.
Mother, Father, and Sam
were sleeping.
So only the cat saw…

At two o'clock in the morning

Amy got up very quietly.

No one else did.

So only the cat saw…

A few hours later
Sam woke Mother.
Amy and Father slept on.
So only the cat saw...

It was breakfast time,
and day had begun.
Mother was washing her face.
Sam was watching Father.
And the cat was sound asleep.
So only Amy saw...

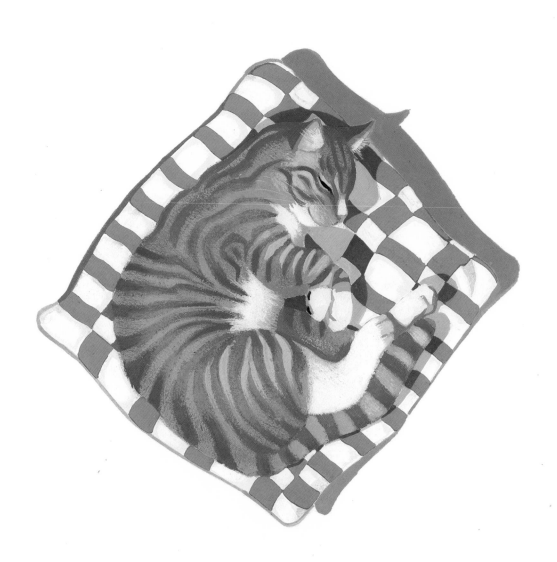

5-13